Zoric the Spaceman

written and illustrated
by PETER KINGSTON

*This story has been adapted
for easy reading
and details are given
on the back endpaper.*

Titles in Series 815

First edition

© LADYBIRD BOOKS LTD MCMLXXXIII

Zoric
tells his story

Ladybird Books Loughborough

One day, Zoric and his friends
were in the forest.

"Tell us about your planet, Zoric," said the snail and the mouse.

So Zoric began to tell the story of his planet and how he landed on Earth.

Zoric's planet was like Earth but everything there was very small.

Zoric was a spaceman.

He had two spaceman friends.
One had an orange coat and shoes.
The other had a blue coat and shoes.

One day the three spacemen were eating their breakfast.

Then the Captain said,
"Enemy spaceships are coming!
Please take off now!"

Zoric and his two friends took off in their spaceships.

"I can see the enemy," said Zoric. "Get ready to attack."

The enemy spaceships came nearer.

"Get ready!" said Zoric, and he and his friends got ready to attack.

WHOOSH! went Zoric's missile.
WHOOSH! WHOOSH! went
the other missiles.

Zoric's missile hit one enemy spaceship.

BANG! BANG! went the other missiles.

The enemy spaceships went away.
"Well done, Zoric!" said one spaceman.

"Zoric! Zoric! Where are you?"
he said. But Zoric was not there.

The spacemen looked everywhere but they could not find Zoric.

They went home to see their Captain. "Well done!" he said. "But why are you sad?"

"We've lost Zoric," they said.
"We cannot find him anywhere."

Then a spaceman on a big television
set said, "I've seen Zoric."

15

"Where is he?" said the Captain.
"He is going to Earth," said the man.

"Zoric will be in danger," said one of
Zoric's friends. "Everything on Earth
is very big."

"Zoric will be all right," said the
Captain. "If he does not come back
soon we will go and rescue him."

Back on Earth, Zoric ended his story.
"So I came to Earth when my
spaceship went wrong!" he said.

"Your friends will think you are in danger," said the mouse and the snail.

"Yes, but I am safe here on Earth with you," said Zoric.

Zoric
returns to
his planet

Back in space, Zoric's friends were getting ready to rescue him.

"Everything is ready," they said.
"We will soon rescue Zoric."

They got into the rescue spaceship
to go to planet Earth.

10..9..8..7..6..5..4..3..2..1
...LIFT OFF!

Soon Zoric's friends and the Captain were in space, on their way to Earth.

Back on Earth, Zoric did not know
that his friends were on their way.
He was painting his house.

"Can I help you?" said the mouse.

"Yes," said Zoric. "You can paint the top of my house."

The mouse went up to the top of the house. But then he started to slip.

The mouse slipped down and down and landed in the red paint.

The mouse had red paint all over him.
Zoric laughed and laughed.

''Oh dear, Mouse,'' he said.
''You must go to the river and wash off the red paint.''

At the same time, Zoric's friends from
space were landing on Earth,
in the forest.

The Captain looked out of the spaceship.
"Everything is very big," he said.

They all got out of the spaceship.
"How will we find Zoric?" they said.

"I can hear something over there!"
said one man.

All the spacemen went to see.

"Look!" they said. "It's a big mouse. Why is he red?"

The mouse was washing off the red paint but the spacemen did not know.

"We must catch the mouse,"
said one spaceman.

"He could know where Zoric is."
He went back to their spaceship.

He came back and gave the Captain a
big net with rockets on it.

The men went back to the river.
"Now we can catch the mouse,"
they said.

"One, two, three, **FIRE**!"
said the Captain.

ZOOM! went the net. It went over the river and over the mouse.

"Help! Let me out!" said the mouse.

The spacemen went into the river to catch the mouse.

"Oh!" said the mouse. "You are all like Zoric!"

"Where is Zoric?" they said. "Have you seen him?"

"Zoric is my friend," said the mouse.
"I was helping him to paint his house."

"Then I slipped and landed in the red paint."

The spacemen took off the net.

"Come with me," said the mouse. "I'll take you to Zoric's house."

When they got there, Zoric had a big surprise.

His friends were very happy to see him.
''Hello, Zoric,'' they said.

"Hello," said Zoric. "I didn't know if I would see you again."

"We thought you would be in danger," the Captain said. "The animals are very big."

The animals looked cross.

"I am not in danger," said Zoric. "The animals are my friends."

"The animals helped me to find this house," said Zoric. "Come and see."

The animals went to get some food for Zoric's friends.

Soon the Captain said, "It is time to go now, Zoric. Are you ready?"

Zoric and the animals looked very sad.

"Don't be sad," said the Captain.
"Zoric will come back to see you."

"But how will Zoric know when we
need him to help us?" said the bird.

The Captain had an idea.
He went back to the spaceship.

Soon he came back with a small television set.

"You can talk to Zoric and see him on this," said the Captain, and he gave it to the animals.

Zoric took all his things from his
spaceship. Then he got into the
rescue ship.

"Goodbye," he said.
"I will come back soon."

WHOOSH! went the spaceship. All
the animals said, "Goodbye, Zoric!"

Zoric looked out. ''My house is painted
and ready for when I come back,''
he said.

His friends laughed and soon they were
in space going back to Zoric's planet.

Notes to parents and teachers

This series of books is designed for children who have begun to read and who need, and will enjoy, wider reading at a supplementary level.

The stories are based on Key Words up to *Level 5c* of the Ladybird Key Words Reading Scheme.

Extra words and words beyond that level are listed below.

Words which the child will meet at *Level 6* are listed separately, in case the parent or teacher wishes to give extra attention to these words and use this series as a bridge between reading levels.

Although based on Key Words, these books are ideal as supplementary reading material for use with any other reading scheme. The high picture content gives visual clues to words which may be unfamiliar and the consistent repetition of new words will give confidence to the reader.

Words used at Level 6

day	very	time
friends	three	bird
tell	find	gave
your	their	
every	dear	